MW00908823

*Nurtured and Nuzzled • Criados y Acariciados*
by Mike Speiser


First Edition • February 2016
Paperback ISBN 13: 978-1-930775-80-0 • ISBN 10: 1-930775-80-6
E-book ISBN 13: 978-1-930775-81-7 • ISBN 10: 1-930775-81-4

Teacher's Guide available

Translation by Dolores Aguilar, Norwalk, CA
Design by Linsey Silver, *Element 47 Design*, Washington, DC

Published by Platypus Media, LLC
725 8th Street SE • Washington, DC 20003
202-546-1674 • Toll-free: 1-877-752-8977
Info@PlatypusMedia.com • www.PlatypusMedia.com

Distributed to the book trade by National Book Network
301-459-3366 • 1-800-462-6420
CustomerCare@NBNbooks.com • www.NBNbooks.com

Library of Congress Control Number 2015935954

10 9 8 7 6 5 4 3 2 1



Printed in the United States of America.

# Nurtured and Nuzzled

# Criados y Acariciados

Babies are groomed

*Los bebés son acicalados*

and guided.

y guiados.

Babies are carried

*Los bebés son cargados*

and cuddled.

y mimados.

Babies are snuggled

*Los bebés son acurrucados*

and sheltered.

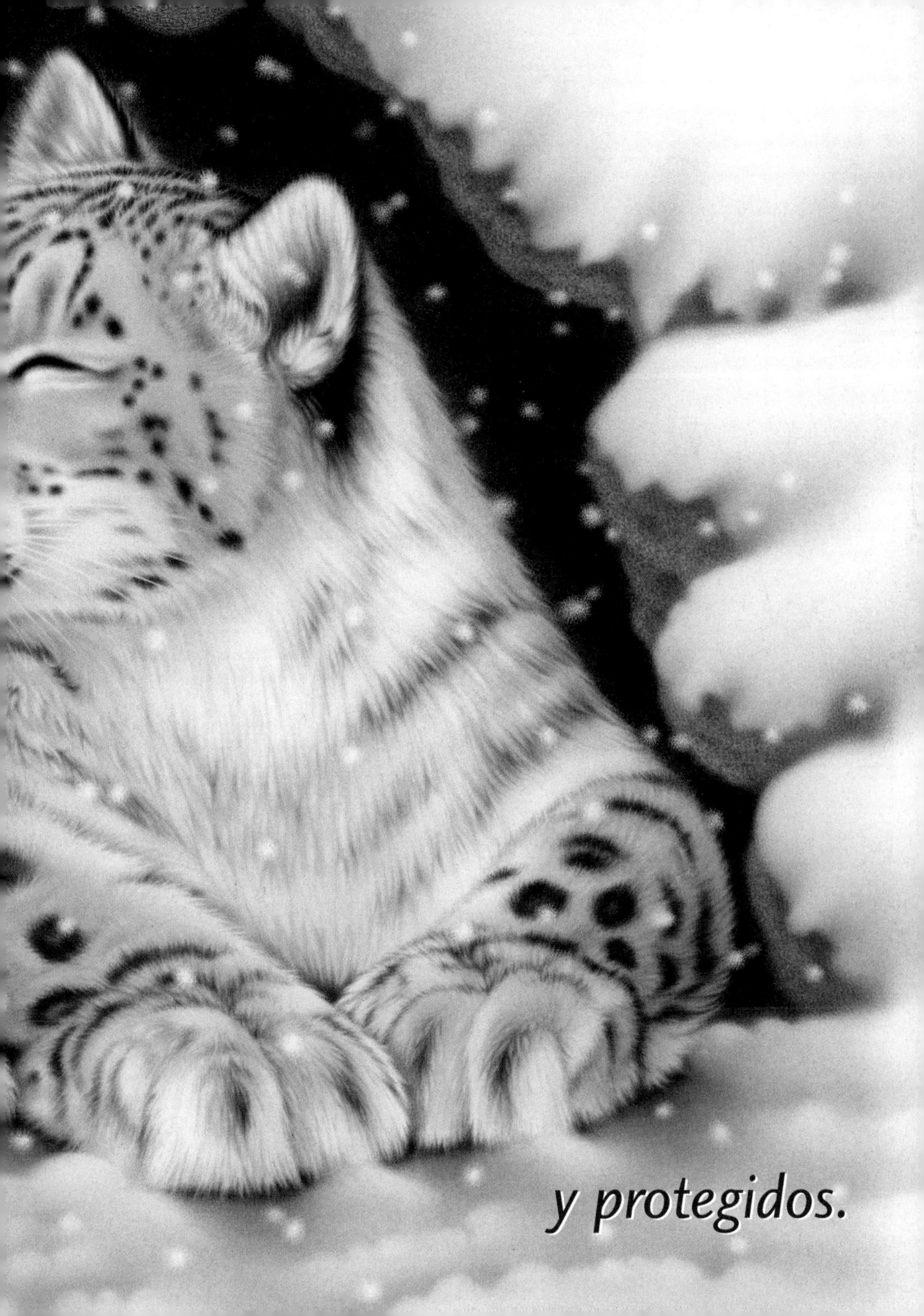

*y protegidos.*

Babies are nurtured

Los bebés son criados

and nuzzled.

*y acariciados.*

# Babies are breastfed

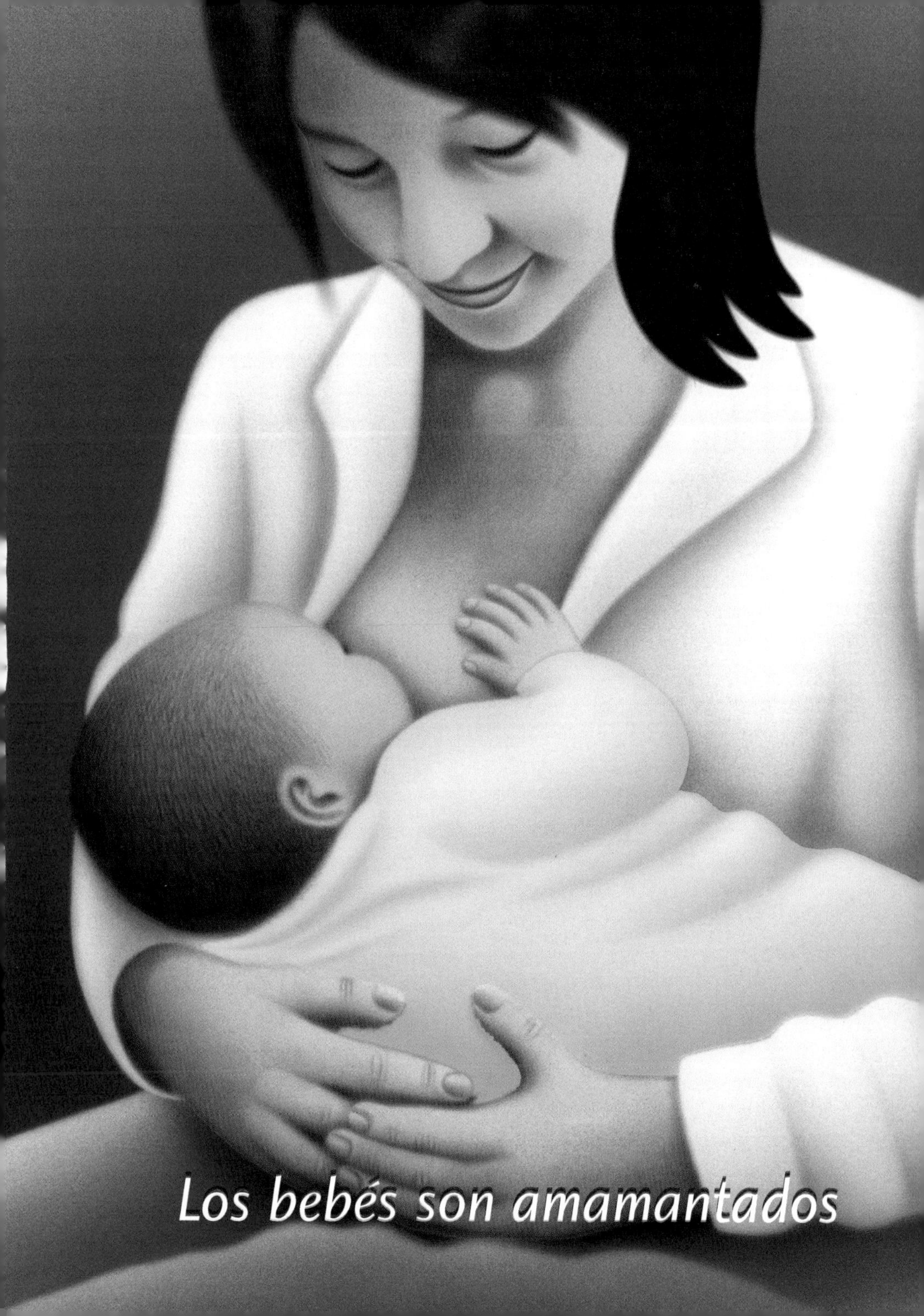

Los bebés son amamantados

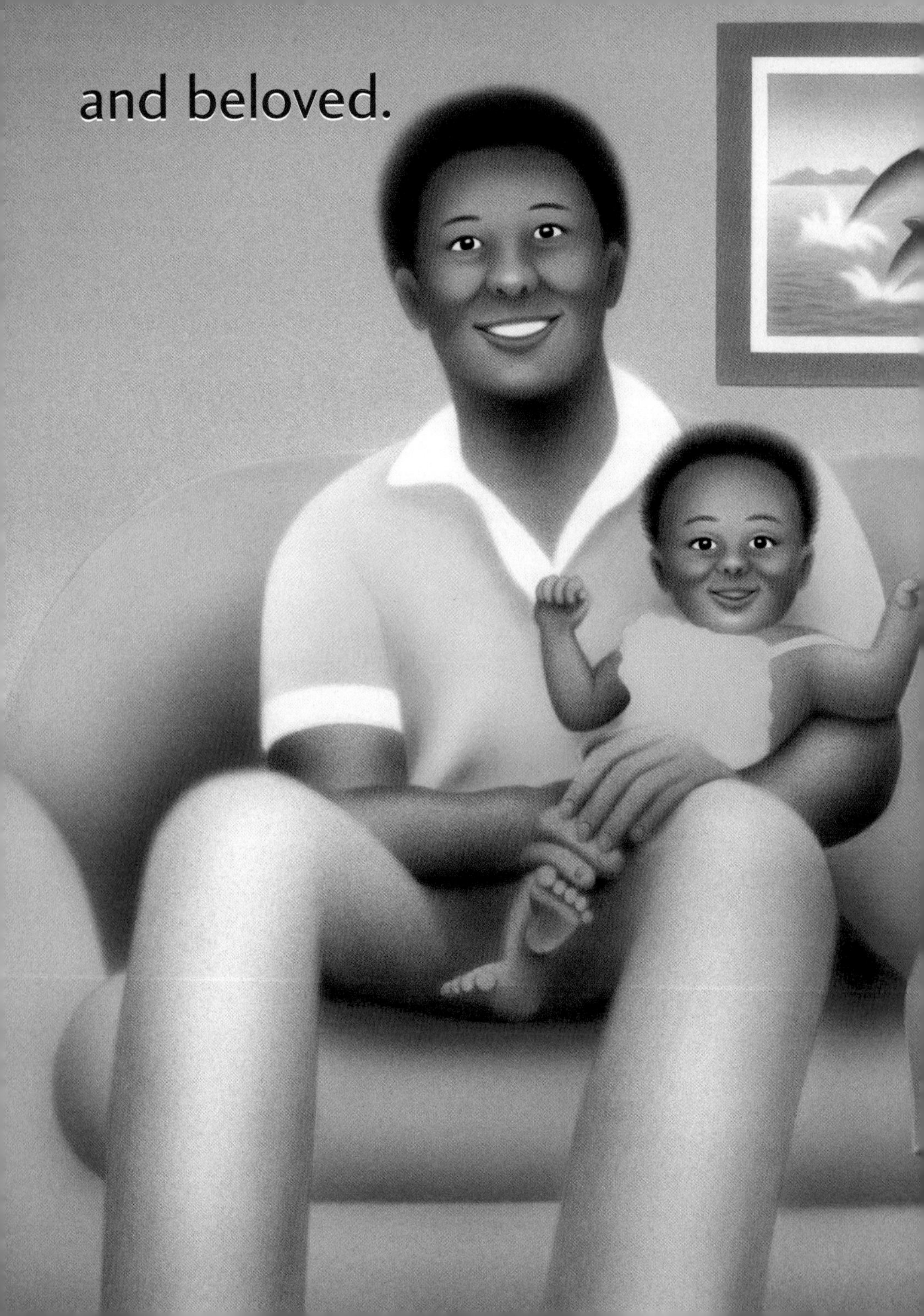

and beloved.

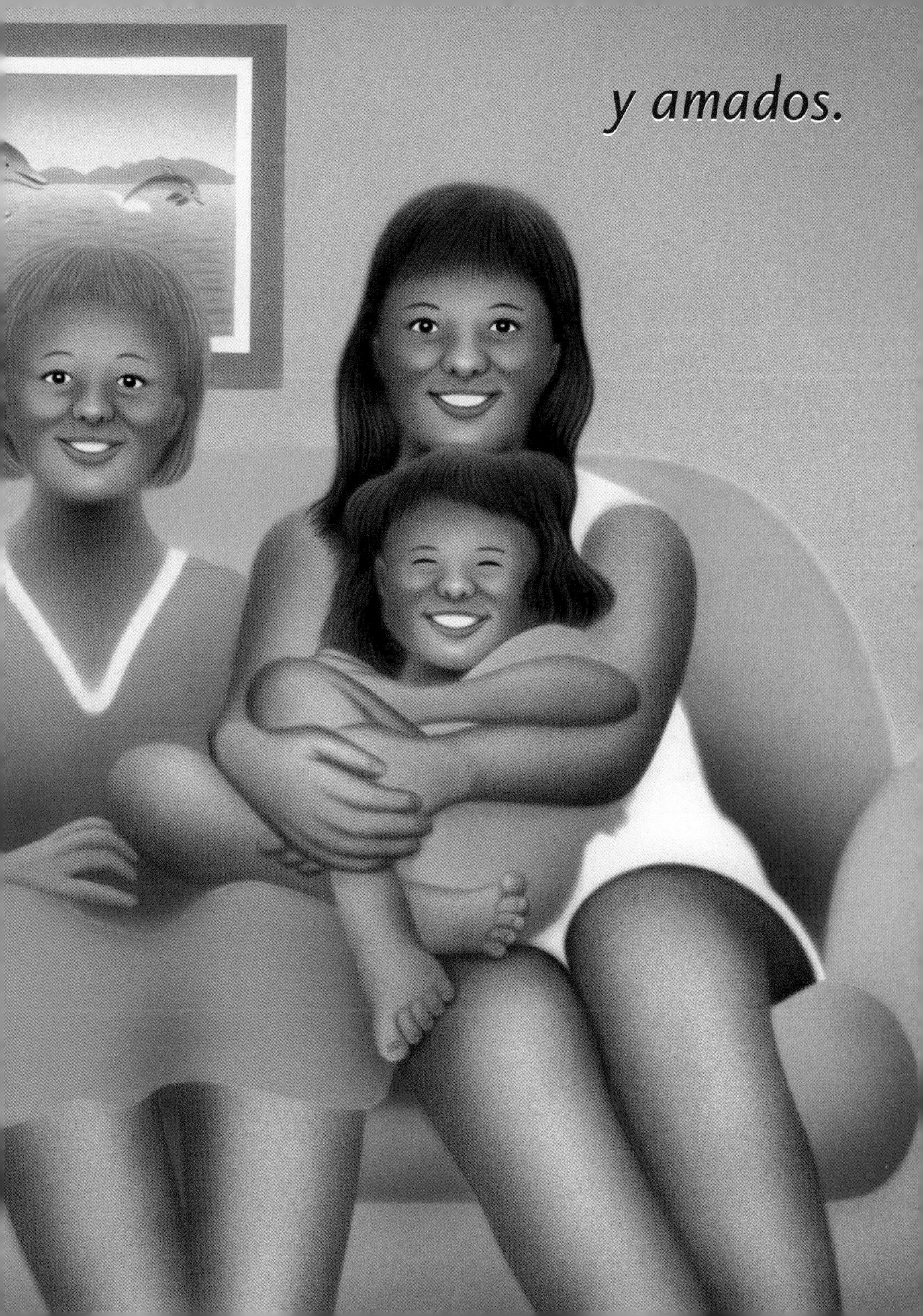

*y amados.*